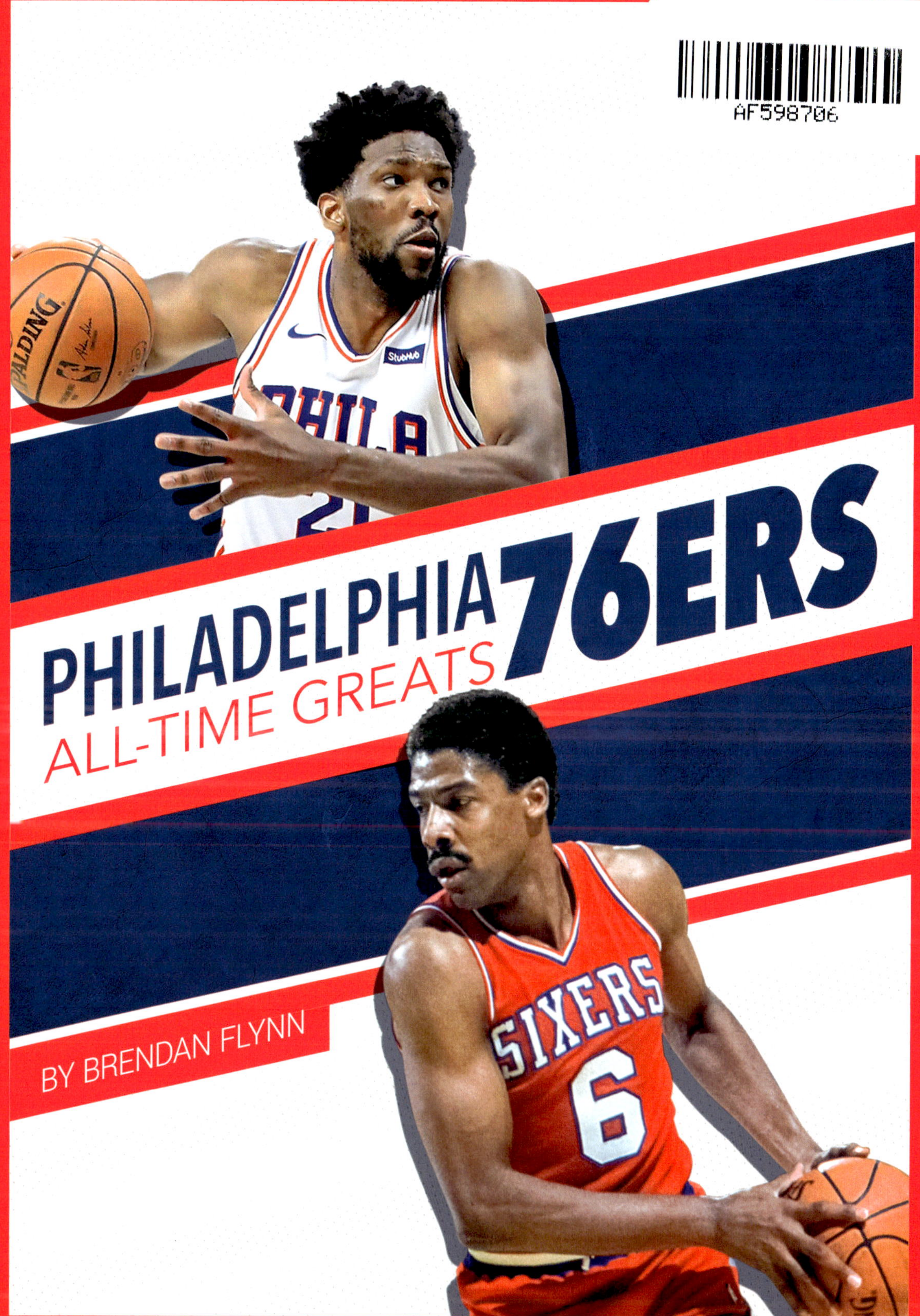

PHILADELPHIA 76ERS
ALL-TIME GREATS

BY BRENDAN FLYNN

Book design by Jake Slavik
Cover design by Jake Slavik

Photographs ©: Andy Lyons/Getty Images Sport/Getty Images, cover (top), 1 (top); John W. McDonough/Icon Sportswire/AP Images, cover (bottom), 1 (bottom); Bettmann/Getty Images, 4; Dick Raphael/Sports Illustrated/Set Number: X13155 TK13 F4/Getty Images, 7; James Drake/Sports Illustrated/Set Number: X21496 TK1/Getty Images, 8; Manny Millan /Sports Illustrated/Set Number: X28565 TK1 R3 F18/Getty Images, 11; Focus on Sport/Getty Images Sport/Getty Images, 12; Steve Lipofsky/Sports Illustrated/Getty Images, 14; Jed Jacobsohn/ Getty Images Sport/Getty Images, 17; Elsa/Getty Images Sport/Getty Images, 18; Mitchell Leff/ Getty Images Sport/Getty Images, 20; Red Line Editorial, 22

Press Box Books, an imprint of Press Room Editions.

ISBN
978-1-63494-158-7 (library bound)
978-1-63494-171-6 (paperback)
978-1-63494-184-6 (epub)
978-1-63494-197-6 (hosted ebook)

Library of Congress Control Number: 2019951062

Distributed by North Star Editions, Inc.
2297 Waters Drive
Mendota Heights, MN 55120
www.northstareditions.com

Printed in the United States of America
012020

ABOUT THE AUTHOR

Brendan Flynn is a San Francisco resident and an author of numerous children's books. In addition to writing about sports, Flynn also enjoys competing in triathlons, Scrabble tournaments, and chili cook-offs.

TABLE OF CONTENTS

SCHAYES
4

CHAPTER 1
PIONEERS

The Philadelphia 76ers are one of the NBA's oldest franchises. But they didn't always play in Philadelphia. They began play in a different league in 1946 as the Syracuse Nationals. They joined the NBA when it formed in 1949 and became a consistently good team. They made the playoffs in each of their 14 NBA seasons. They also won the league title in 1955.

The Nationals' biggest star was center **Dolph Schayes**. He was an ace shooter and strong rebounder. He also served one season as player-coach when the team moved to Philadelphia in 1963.

Another star who spent his entire career with the team was guard **Hal Greer**. He arrived in Syracuse as a second-round pick in the 1958 NBA Draft. He quickly became a solid contributor. Greer was known for his accurate

HAPPY HOMECOMING

Philadelphia native **Wilt Chamberlain** starred for the hometown Warriors. But the team moved to San Francisco in 1962. They traded Chamberlain to the 76ers in January 1965. He led the NBA in rebounding the next three seasons. In the 1967 NBA Finals, Chamberlain and the 76ers beat the San Francisco Warriors to win the NBA title.

STAT SPOTLIGHT

CAREER GAMES

76ERS TEAM RECORD

Hal Greer: 1,122

jump shot from the top of the key. He could also get to the basket on the dribble.

When the team moved to Philadelphia, Greer really took off. He averaged more than 20 points per game in his first seven seasons as a 76er. The 10-time All-Star finally retired in 1973 after a 15-year career as one of the league's top guards.

ERVING
6
SIXERS
6
20

CHAPTER 2

CHAMPIONS

Few players thrilled basketball fans the way **Julius Erving** did. "Dr. J" spent five seasons in the American Basketball Association (ABA) before joining the Sixers in 1976. Already 26 years old, the high-flying forward continued to dominate for another decade.

Erving's graceful drives and powerful dunks filled highlight reels. He also averaged at least 20 points per game in his first nine seasons with the Sixers. He won the NBA Most Valuable Player (MVP) Award in 1981. Two years later, Dr. J led the way as the Sixers brought the NBA championship back to Philadelphia. It was their first title in 16 years.

In September 1982, the 76ers made a trade that gave Dr. J the help he needed to win that title. Bruising center **Moses Malone** was the reigning NBA MVP. He'd averaged 31.1 points and 14.7 rebounds per game for the Houston Rockets. In Philadelphia, Malone won a second straight MVP trophy and the Sixers dominated the league. They posted a 65–17 record in the regular season. Then they cruised through the playoffs, losing just one game along the way.

MVP MALONE

Malone did more than just win back-to-back NBA MVP Awards. He was named NBA Finals MVP after the Sixers swept the Lakers in 1983. He led the Sixers in scoring in all four games and averaged 18 rebounds per game in the series.

MALONE
2
SIXERS
2
RAMBIS
31
PORTER

CHEEKS
10
SIXERS
10
NEW YORK
4

The 1983 title team had its share of unsung heroes too. Point guard **Maurice Cheeks** was a first-team All-Defensive pick four straight seasons. He shut down opposing guards while directing the Philadelphia offense. He also averaged 12.2 points per game during his 11 seasons with the 76ers.

The championship-winning coach was a former Sixers player. **Billy Cunningham** was a star forward on Philadelphia's 1967 championship team. He was just 34 when he took over as the team's head coach in 1977–78. In the next six years the 76ers won the Eastern Conference three times.

STAT SPOTLIGHT

CAREER ASSISTS

76ERS TEAM RECORD

Maurice Cheeks: 6,212

BARKLEY
34
SIXERS
34

CHAPTER 3
SUPERSTARS

The 76ers suffered a long title drought after that 1983 championship. But they've had plenty of exciting players since then. One of the most familiar faces in the league got his start in Philadelphia. **Charles Barkley** never had the typical body of an NBA superstar. But he sure played like one.

The bulky Barkley was a double-double machine. In fact, he averaged more than 10 rebounds per game in 15 of his 16 NBA seasons. And he scored 20 points per game in 11 straight seasons. Barkley was always quick with a witty quote. Today, he might be known more as an NBA broadcaster.

Barkley left Philadelphia in 1992. Four years later, **Allen Iverson** arrived to fill the superstar void. The dynamic young guard took the league by storm. He led the league in scoring four times in his first nine years with the Sixers. Iverson won the 2001 NBA MVP Award after leading the 76ers to the NBA Finals for the first time since 1983.

Iverson often used his unstoppable crossover dribble to get to the basket. Once he was in the lane, he was fearless. He threw his body into traffic and usually came away with the basket. He was tireless too, leading the NBA in minutes per game seven times.

STAT SPOTLIGHT

SINGLE-SEASON STEALS

76ERS TEAM RECORD

Allen Iverson: 225 (2002-03)

EMBIID
21

CHAPTER 4
MODERN STARS

The 76ers endured a long stretch as the worst team in the league. They averaged fewer than 20 wins per season over a four-year span that ended in 2017. However, they drafted wisely and came away with a handful of potential superstars.

Center **Joel Embiid** proved he was worth the wait. After he played just one season in college, the Sixers selected him third in the 2014 NBA Draft. Multiple foot injuries kept him off the court for the next two seasons. Once he returned, a knee injury limited him

to just 31 games his rookie year. But he was still named to the NBA All-Rookie first team. He averaged 20.2 points and 7.8 rebounds per game that year.

Embiid steadily improved those numbers. He posted 27.5 points and 13.6 rebounds per game in 2018–19, his second straight All-Star season. He also became one of the best three-point shooters among NBA big men.

Point guard **Ben Simmons** was the first pick in the 2016 draft. He missed the next season with a foot injury. But he returned to win the NBA Rookie of the Year Award with a strong all-around game. In his first two NBA seasons, Simmons averaged 16.4 points, 8.5 rebounds, and 7.9 assists per game. He helped the Sixers advance to the Eastern Conference semifinals in each of his first two seasons.

PHILLY ROOTS

Swingman **Andre Iguodala** won multiple championships with the Golden State Warriors. But he got his start in Philadelphia. Iguodala was the Sixers' first-round pick in the 2004 draft and played his first eight seasons with them.

TIMELINE

1949
1950
DOLPH SCHAYES
(1949-50 TO 1963-64)
1960
HAL GREER
(1958-59 TO 1972-73)
WILT CHAMBERLAIN
(1965 TO 1967-68)
BILLY CUNNINGHAM
(1965-66 TO 1971-72;
1974-75 TO 1975-76)
1970
JULIUS ERVING
(1976-77 TO 1986-87)
1980
MAURICE CHEEKS
(1978-79 TO 1988-89)
MOSES MALONE
(1982-83 TO 1985-86;
1993-94)
CHARLES BARKLEY
(1984-85 TO 1991-92)
1990
ALLEN IVERSON
(1996-97 TO 2006;
2009-10)
2000
ANDRE IGUODOLA
(2004-05 TO 2011-12)
2010
JOEL EMBIID
(2016-17 TO PRESENT)
BEN SIMMONS
(2017-18 TO PRESENT)
2020

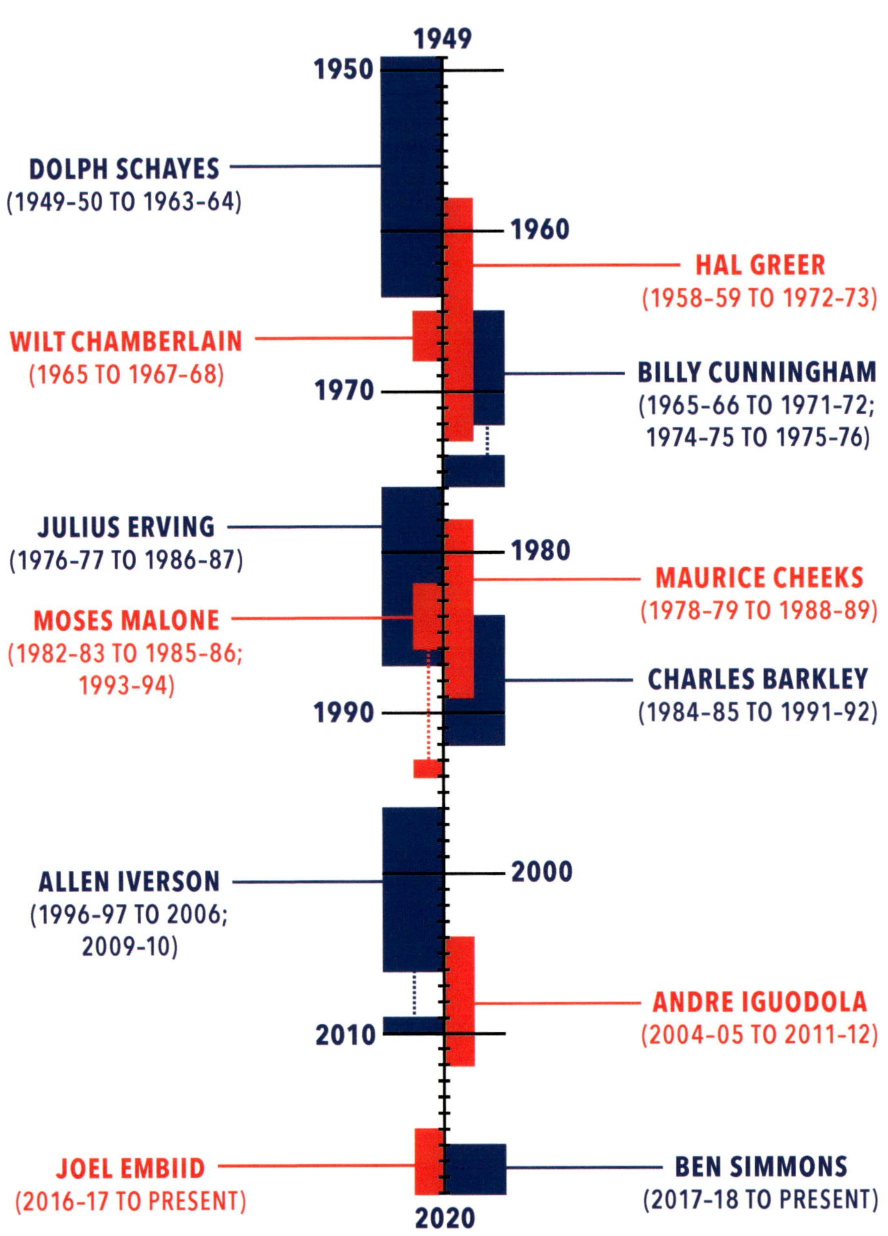

TEAM FACTS

PHILADELPHIA 76ERS

Formerly: Syracuse Nationals (1949–50 to 1962–63)

First season: 1949–50

NBA championships: 3*

Key coaches:

Al Cervi (1949–50 to 1956–57)
294–201, 33–26 playoffs, 1 NBA title

Billy Cunningham (1977–78 to 1984–85)
454–196, 66–39 playoffs, 1 NBA title

Alex Hannum (1960–61 to 1962–63, 1966–67 to 1967–68)
257–145, 26–20 playoffs, 1 NBA title

MORE INFORMATION

To learn more about the Philadelphia 76ers, go to **pressboxbooks.com/AllAccess.**

These links are routinely monitored and updated to provide the most current information available.

**Through 2018–19 season*

GLOSSARY

assist
A pass that leads directly to a basket.

crossover
A dribble that moves quickly from one hand to the other, allowing the dribbler space to drive to the hoop.

double-double
Accumulating 10 or more of two certain statistics in a game.

drought
A prolonged period without success.

dynamic
Energetic, creating positive change.

franchise
A sports organization.

key
The free-throw lane and the free-throw circle together.

reigning
Having most recently won an award.

rookie
A first-year player.

unsung
Rarely praised or given credit.

void
Gap or empty space.

INDEX